CU00841098

ISBN 1-84135-194-6

Copyright © 2003 Award Publications Limited

First published 2003

Published by Award Publications Limited,
27 Longford Street, London NW1 3DZ

Printed in Malaysia

Award Young Readers

Henny Penny

Rewritten by Jackie Andrews
Illustrated by Lawrie Taylor

AWARD PUBLICATIONS LIMITED

One day, Henny Penny was picking up corn in the farmyard when – *whack*! An acorn fell and hit her on the head.

"Oh dear me!" said Henny Penny. "The sky is falling. I must go and tell the king."

Off she went down the road and on the way met Cocky Locky, who said, "Good morning, Henny Penny. Where are you going this fine day?"

"I'm going to tell the king that the sky is falling," said Henny Penny. "A piece of it fell on my head."

"May I go, too?" asked Cocky Locky.
Henny Penny answered, "Come along,"
and they set off together to find the king.

They went past trees and past houses and soon they met Ducky Lucky waddling down the dusty road.

"Good morning, Henny Penny and Cocky Locky," said Ducky Lucky. "Where are you going this fine day?"

"We're going to tell the king that the sky is falling," said Henny Penny. "A piece of it fell on my head."

"May I go, too?" Ducky Lucky asked.
"Come along then," said Henny Penny, and
they all set off together to find the king.

They passed a man on a horse and a man with a dog and soon they met Goosey Loosey hurrying along down the dusty road,

"Good morning, friends. Where are you going this fine day?" asked Goosey Loosey.

"We're going to tell the king that the sky is falling," said Henny Penny. "A piece of it fell on my head."

"May I go with you?" asked Goosey Loosey.

"Come along then," said Henny Penny, and they set off together to find the king.

They went through a gate and behind a church and soon they met Turkey Lurkey coming along down the dusty road.

"Good morning. Where are you going?" asked Turkey Lurkey.

"We're going to tell the king the sky is falling," said Henny Penny. "A piece of it fell on my head."

Turkey Lurkey asked, "May I go, too?"

Henny Penny said, "Come along then," and they all went off together to find the king.

They crossed a bridge and went over hills and soon met Foxy Woxy coming down the road.

"Good morning," said Foxy Woxy. "Where are you all going this fine day?"

Henny Penny answered, "We're on our way to tell the king that the sky is falling. A piece of it fell on my head."

"May I go, too?" asked Foxy Woxy.
Henny Penny said, "Come along then,"
and they all set off together to find the king.

Suddenly Foxy Woxy stopped in the middle of the road and said, "Oh, dear me, this isn't the best way to the castle. I know a much shorter route. Would you like me to show it to you?"

"That would be very kind of you, Foxy Woxy," said Henny Penny, Cocky Locky, Ducky Lucky, Goosey Loosey, and Turkey Lurkey.

They all went along together to
tell the king that the sky was falling.

They went past trees and more trees, and
finally they came to a dark hole where Foxy Woxy
lived, but he did not tell them so.

Foxy Woxy said, "Here is the short cut to the
king's castle. We'll soon get there if you follow
me. I'll go first and you come after me, one at
a time – Turkey Lurkey, Goosey Loosey, Ducky
Lucky, Cocky Locky, and then Henny Penny."

Foxy Woxy led the way into his hole,
and waited for them to follow.

And they did. Just as he told them. Turkey Lurkey went in first, and he had not gone very far before Foxy Woxy gobbled him up.

Goosey Loosey went in next, and she had not gone very far before Foxy Woxy gobbled her up, too.

Ducky Lucky went next. He had not gone very far either before Foxy Woxy gobbled him up as well.

Then Cocky Locky went in. But as soon as he saw Foxy Woxy, he realised what had happened and called out to Henny Penny very loudly.

Henny Penny ran home as fast as she could.

And so Henny Penny never got to tell the king that the sky was falling, after all.